For Edie, the best treat of all, and for Janine O'Malley,
great to work with on Halloween and every other day of the year —A.W.P.

Especially for Anna —D.W.

Farrar Straus Giroux Books for Young Readers
An imprint of Macmillan Publishing Group, LLC
120 Broadway, New York, NY 10271
mackids.com

Our books may be purchased in bulk for promotional, educational, or business use. Please contact your local bookseller or the Macmillan Corporate and
Premium Sales Department at (800) 221-7945 ext. 5442 or by email at MacmillanSpecialMarkets@macmillan.com.

Library of Congress Cataloging-in-Publication Data
Names: Paul, Ann Whitford, author. | Walker, David, 1965– illustrator.
Title: If animals trick-or-treated / Ann Whitford Paul ; pictures by David Walker.
Description: First edition. | New York: Farrar Straus Giroux, 2022. | Audience: Ages 2–6. | Audience: Grades K–1. | Summary: Illustrations and simple,
rhyming text explores what would happen if animals celebrated Halloween.
Identifiers: LCCN 2020039530 | ISBN 9780374388522 (hardcover)
Subjects: CYAC: Stories in rhyme. | Halloween—Fiction. | Animals—Habits and behavior—Fiction.
Classification: LCC PZ8.3.P273645 Ifk 2022 | DDC [E]—dc23
LC record available at https://lccn.loc.gov/2020039530

First edition, 2022
Book design by Melisa Vuong
Color separations by Bright Arts (H.K.) Ltd.
Printed in China by Toppan Leefung Printing Ltd., Dongguan City, Guangdong Province

ISBN 978-0-374-38852-2 (hardcover)
1 3 5 7 9 10 8 6 4 2

If Animals Trick-or-Treated

Ann Whitford Paul

Pictures by David Walker

Farrar Straus Giroux

New York

If animals trick-or-treated,

Mama and Owlet at the pumpkin stall
would first choose a pumpkin like Owlet—small.

They'd carve two round eyes and two pointy ears.

Bat Pup would carve hers with fangs like spears.

Hatchling would beg Papa Crocodile
to carve his pumpkin a **sneee-eeery** smile.

If animals trick-or-treated,
then Mama and Owlet would
decorate trees
with cobwebs
swish-swaying
in the breeze.

Anteater and Pup would shove with their snouts
to **loop-de-loop** orange and black streamers about.

Vulture Chicks would **scat-scatter** fresh skeleton bones close to a cluster of old tombstones.

If animals trick-or-treated,
Owlet would fly in his super-bird cape.
Piglet would waddle in mummy tape.

Zebra Foal would **prance-prance** in a costume of spots.
Little Leopard would run wearing stripes—lots and lots!

Panther would don a tall witchy hat
and hold paws with her spooky black cub cat.

If animals trick-or-treated,

Owlet and friends would

knock-knock-knock

at nests, outside dens, and under a rock,
promising a trick if they didn't get treats.

Parrot would give out her **yummy** seed sweets.

Armadillo would offer chocolate ants.

Elephant?

Candied leafy plants.

Bear's surprise?

Honey gummy bears.

Raccoon?

His famous garbage-fudge squares.

Then stuffed to his beak with no room for more,
Owlet would **flap-flap** his wings and soar . . .

. . . to Mama.
Under the moon's spooky light,
they'd read scary stories and shiver
with fright,

but sitting close,
feather to feather,
they'd feel brave,
cozy together.